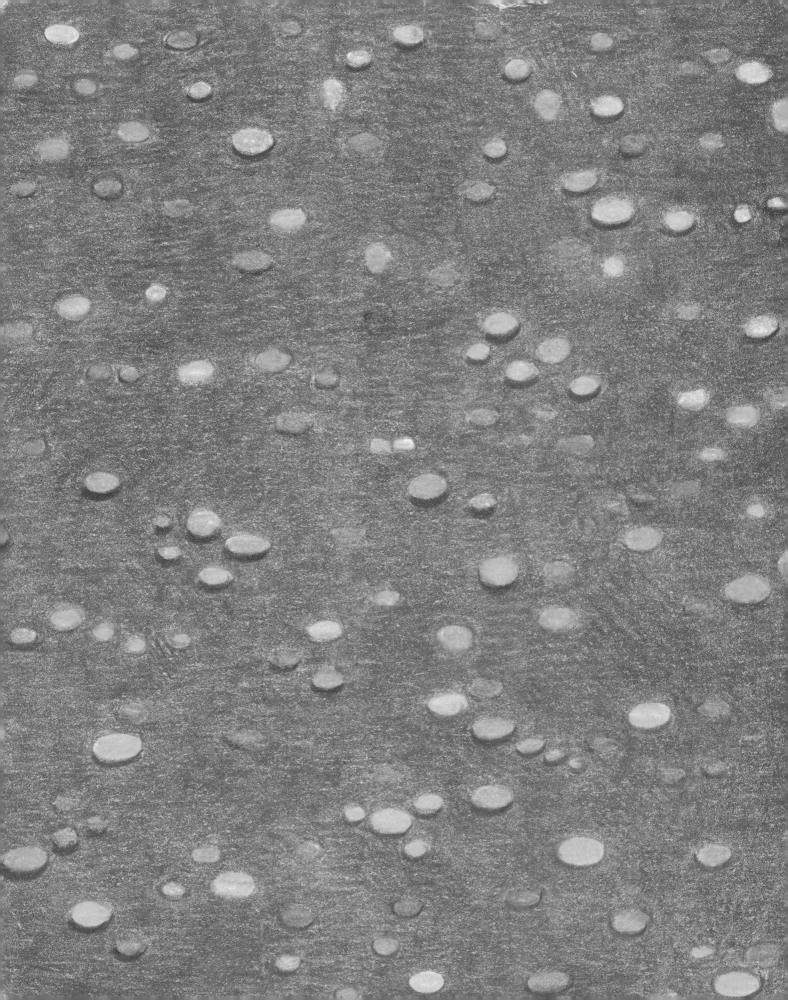

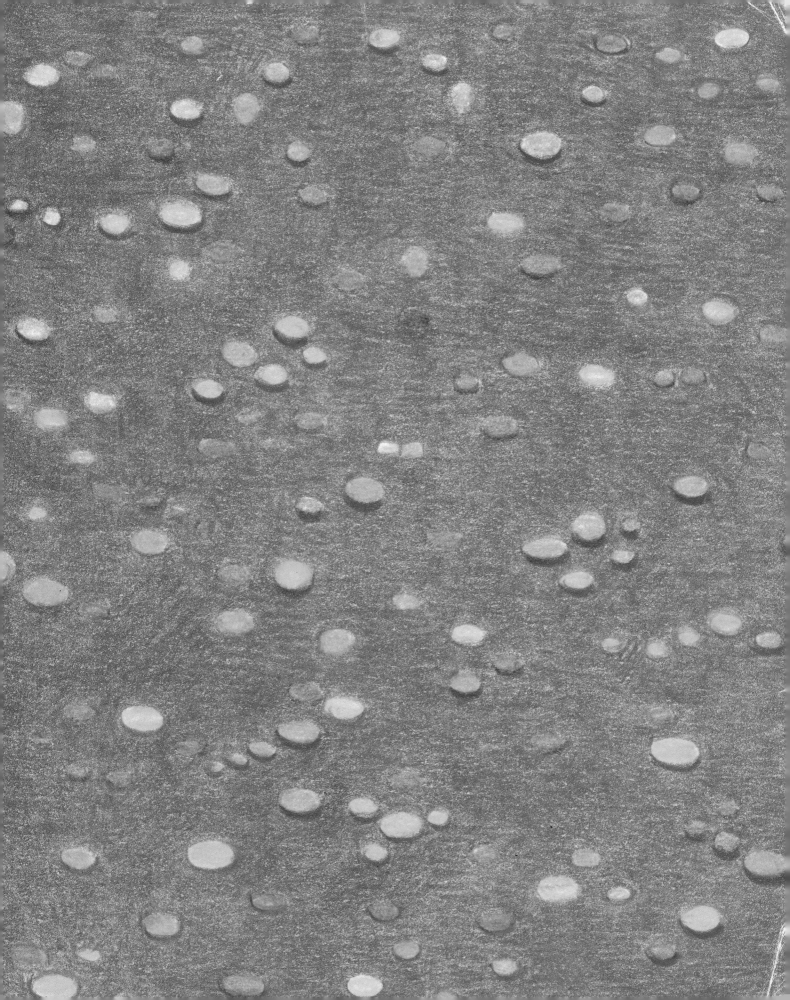

For Sharmon, Nathene and Christine

Old Bear and Friends by Jane Hissey in Red Fox

Old Bear Little Bear's Trousers Little Bear Lost
Jolly Tall Jolly Snow Ruff Hoot
Old Bear and His Friends Old Bear Tales Little Bear's Dragon
Little Bear's Alphabet Little Bear's Numbers

OLD BEAR'S ALL-TOGETHER PAINTING
A RED FOX BOOK 0 09 941313 2

First published in Great Britain by Hutchinson,
an imprint of Random House Children's Books

Hutchinson edition published 2001
Red Fox edition published 2002

1 3 5 7 9 10 8 6 4 2

Red Fox Books are published by Random House Children's Books,
61–63 Uxbridge Road, London W5 5SA, a division of The Random House Group Ltd,
in Australia by Random House Australia (Pty) Ltd, 20 Alfred Street, Milsons Point, Sydney, NSW 2061, Australia,
in New Zealand by Random House New Zealand Ltd, 18 Poland Road, Glenfield, Auckland 10, New Zealand,
and in South Africa by Random House (Pty) Ltd, Endulini, 5A Jubilee Road, Parktown 2193, South Africa

THE RANDOM HOUSE GROUP Limited Reg. No. 954009
www.randomhouse.co.uk

A CIP catalogue record for this book is available from the British Library.

Printed in Singapore by Tien Wah Press PTE Ltd

Old Bear's All-Together Painting

Jane Hissey

RED FOX

Old Bear had been busy all afternoon painting a picture. 'I found this tiny frame,' he told the other toys. 'My painting of Little Bear will just fit in nicely.'

'I want to
paint a picture
too,' said Little Bear. 'Are there any more frames?'
'There's a big one,' said Old Bear. 'Why don't you all paint a picture together. That would be fun.'

'I want to do my *own* painting,' said Little Bear, 'all by myself.'

'So do I,' said Rabbit.

'And me,' barked Ruff.

'Old Bear could choose one to go in the big frame,' said Jolly Tall.

'But what shall we paint?' asked Duck. 'We can't *all* do pictures of Little Bear.'

'I don't see why not,' said Little Bear.

‘I think I’ll paint a ball,’ said Ruff, ‘or a spaceship or maybe a house . . .’

‘Or just a pattern,’ suggested Little Bear.

‘Why don’t we *all* do patterns?’ said Rabbit. ‘I think I’ll paint stripes.’

He dipped two brushes in the paint and bounced along the paper, painting lines as he went.

'Oh dear!' he sighed when he reached the end. 'My stripes are all wavy.'

‘That’s because you bounce up and down, up and down when you run,’ laughed Bramwell Brown.

Meanwhile Jolly had painted a row of orange dots.
'This is my spotty pattern,' he said proudly.

But the paint was much too runny. The toys watched as it dribbled all the way down to the bottom of the paper.

‘Your spots have turned into stripes,’ said Duck.

‘And they’re straighter stripes than mine,’ said Rabbit.

Little Bear was waving his paint brush above his head.
'Look,' he cried, 'I can make hundreds of spots.
My paper is covered in them.'
'And so are you,' laughed the other toys.

'I'm doing GIANT spots,' barked Ruff.

He bounced his rubber ball into the paint pot, then onto the paper.

SPLODGE!

It made a big splattered blob of yellow.

‘That’s fun,’ cried Little Bear. ‘Do it again.’

But this time the ball missed the paper and landed SPLASH in the water.

‘Oh, Ruff,’ cried Duck, ‘now there are puddles all over my painting.’

‘Sorry,’ said Ruff, dabbing the splashes with a cloth. ‘Is that better?’

‘It isn’t quite the pattern I wanted,’ grumbled Duck.

'It's lovely!' said Old Bear, as he arrived to collect the paintings. 'In fact, all your patterns are perfect.'

'*I* don't think so,' said Duck, staring at the dribbles and splodges and wiggly lines.

'Just wait and see,' called Old Bear, as he hurried away.

The toys were still clearing away the painting things when Old Bear returned a little later.

'Now cover your eyes and come with me,' he said, 'and no peeping till we're there!'

Old Bear led the toys to a large picture propped against the wall. 'Now you can look,' he said.

They all stared in amazement.
'Oh, its lovely,' cried
Little Bear. 'Who did it?'

'You all did,' laughed Old Bear. 'I just cut out your patterns and stuck them together. Look, Jolly's orange stripes are the boat and Rabbit's wavy lines are the sea.'

'So Ruff's yellow splodge is the sun,' said Duck, 'and I must have painted the sky.'

'I can see my spots,' cried Little Bear, 'on the sails of the boat.'

'That's right,' said Old Bear, 'and you all did the patterns on the fish.'

‘I see,’ said Little Bear. ‘So we did do an all-together painting after all. That was fun!’

‘I said it would be,’ laughed Old Bear.

'And now, after all
our hard work,
let's have an
all-together tea!'

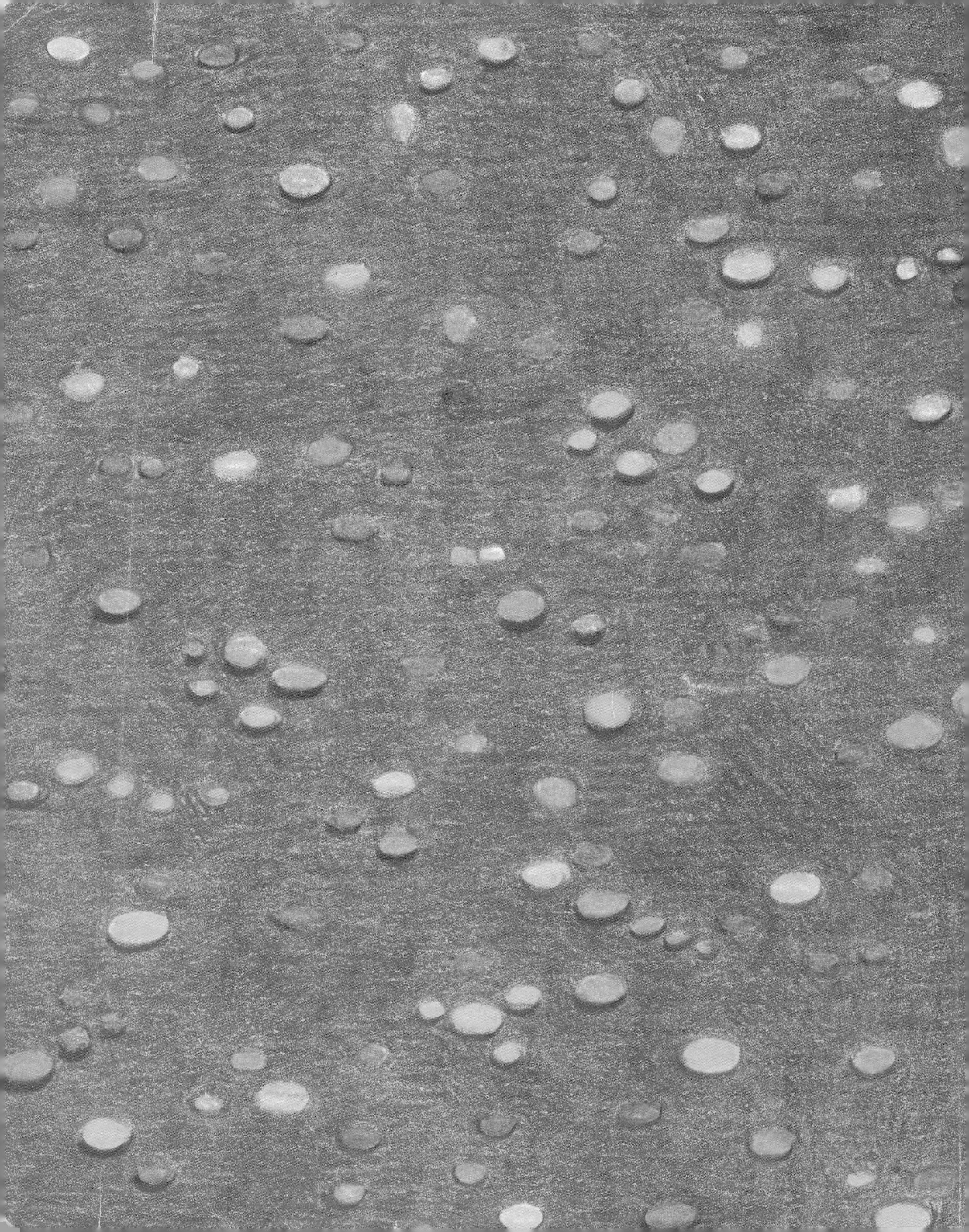

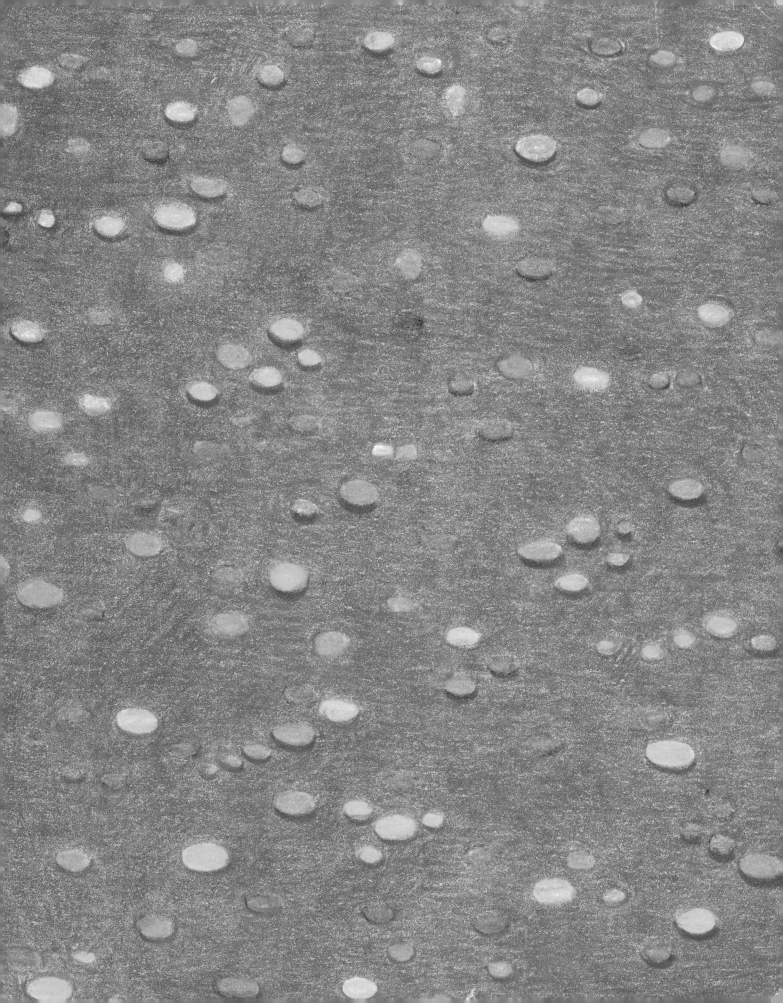